Cloud Boy

Cloud Boy

Rhode Montijo

SIMON AND SCHUSTER
New York London Sydney

High up in the sky
lived a lonely little cloud boy.

One day a butterfly wandered high
into the clouds.

The lonely little cloud boy felt
lucky to see such a beautiful
thing. Then he had an idea...

He gathered the fluff
from a nearby cloud and
made his own butterfly.

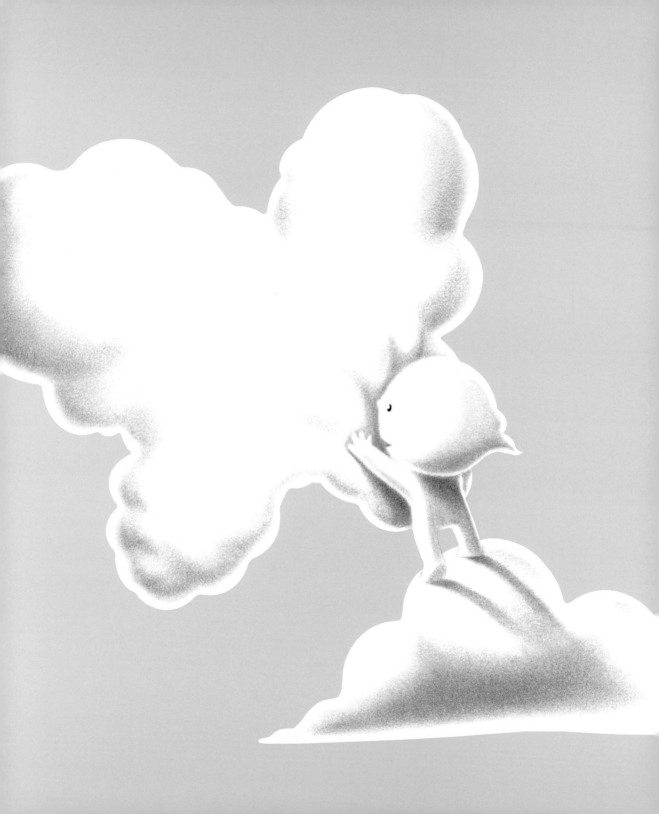

He sent it off for others to see.

The lonely little cloud
boy looked at the
world below and saw
more wondrous things.

He looked at the clouds above and
imagined what they could be.

He was so inspired.

He made big things.

And he made little things.

Soon the sky was filled
with his fluffy creations!

And the little cloud boy knew
that he would never be lonely again.

For Mom and Dad

SIMON AND SCHUSTER
First published in Great Britain in 2006 by Simon & Schuster UK Ltd
Africa House, 64-78 Kingsway, London WC2B 6AH

Originally published in 2006 by Simon and Schuster Books for Young Readers
an imprint of Simon & Schuster Children's Publishing Division, New York

Book design by Daniel Roode
The text for this book is set in Secret Recipe and Bookman Old Style

A CIP catalogue record for this book is available from the British Library upon request

ISBN 1-416-91658-X

Printed in China

1 3 5 7 9 8 6 4 2